W9-AQM-825

Mike and Trollee in Trouble

adapted by Maggie Testa
based on the screenplay "Mike the Knight and
Trollee in Trouble" written by Tom Stevenson

Ready-to-Read

Simon Spotlight

New York   London   Toronto   Sydney   New Delhi

SIMON SPOTLIGHT
An imprint of Simon & Schuster Children's Publishing Division
1230 Avenue of the Americas, New York, New York 10020
© 2013 Hit (MTK) Limited. Mike the Knight™ and logo and Be a Knight, Do It Right!™
are trademarks of Hit (MTK) Limited. Nickelodeon and all related titles and logos are
trademarks of Viacom International Inc. A different adaptation of this episode was previously
published as *Mike the Knight and Trollee in Trouble* in 2012 in Great Britain
by Simon & Schuster UK Ltd.
For information about special discounts for bulk purchases, please contact Simon & Schuster
Special Sales at 1-866-506-1949 or business@simonandschuster.com.
The Simon & Schuster Speakers Bureau can bring authors to your live event. For more information
or to book an event contact the Simon & Schuster Speakers Bureau at 1-866-248-3049 or visit our
website at www.simonspeakers.com.
Manufactured in the United States of America 1112 LAK
First Edition 10 9 8 7 6 5 4 3 2 1
ISBN 978-1-4424-7334-8 (pbk)
ISBN 978-1-4424-7335-5 (hc)
ISBN 978-1-4424-7336-2 (eBook)

Mike is a knight.

He wants to be brave

and bold in a daring rescue.

Today Mike is playing
with Sparkie and Squirt.
Tickle, tickle, tickle!

Look! It is Mike's sister, Evie.

She needs to find some pepper

to help rescue Trollee.

He is stuck in a tree!

Mike does not know why
he was not asked
to rescue Trollee.
Knights know all about
rescuing.

That is it!

Mike will use his knightly

skills to rescue Trollee!

Mike puts on his armor.

He climbs on his

trusty horse, Galahad.

He pulls out . . . a feather?

Mike reaches Trollee. "Did you bring the pepper?" asks Trollee.

"No," says Mike. "I have knightly things to help rescue you."

Mike will **pull** Trollee out of the tree. Squirt grabs a vine, but it is not long enough!

"We can make it longer!"

says Mike.

"Just tie another vine

to that one."

Mike tries to teach Squirt how to tie a Knight's Knightly Rescue Knot, but Squirt gets stuck!

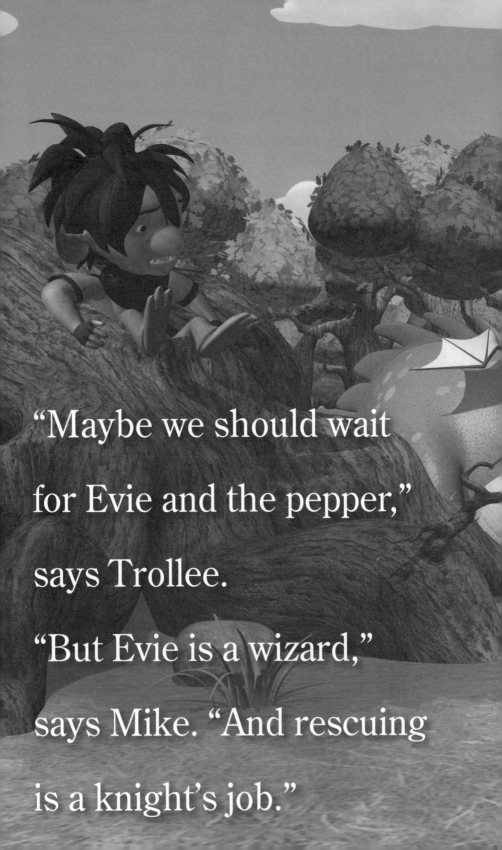

"Maybe we should wait for Evie and the pepper," says Trollee.

"But Evie is a wizard," says Mike. "And rescuing is a knight's job."

Mike will **pop** Trollee

out of the tree!

But it does not work.

Now Sparkie is stuck too.

Mike will have to rescue

Trollee by himself.

But Mike gets
stuck too!

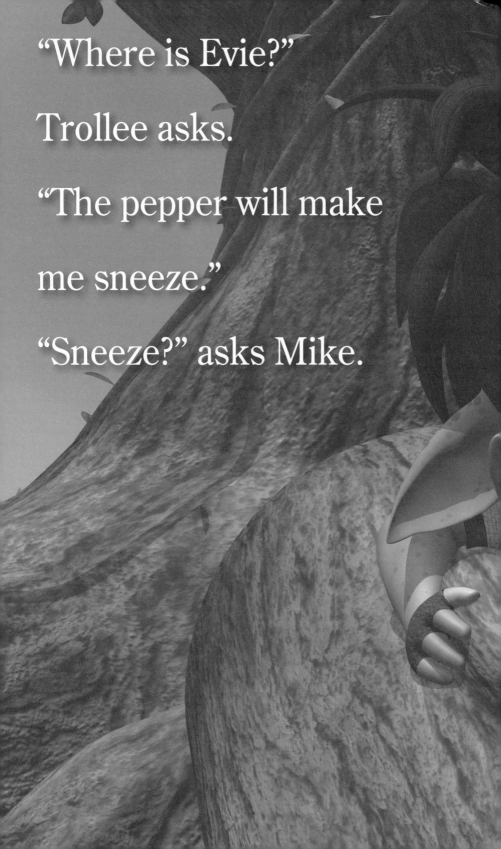

"Where is Evie?" Trollee asks.

"The pepper will make me sneeze."

"Sneeze?" asks Mike.

"Yes," says Trollee. "Sneezing will help me wriggle my way out!"

Dust will make Trollee
sneeze too.
Mike asks Sparkie to flap his
wings and make a dust cloud.

"Hold your nose!"

Mike tells Sparkie

so he does not sneeze.

When Sparkie sneezes,

he blows fire!

Trollee and Mike are free!

The dragons are still stuck.

"It is time to be a knight

and do it right!" says Mike.

He uses his feather to

tickle the dragons.

They wriggle and get free too!

Huzzah!